The
HUNTER

Paul Geraghty

CROWN PUBLISHERS, INC.

New York

The
HUNTER

Paul Geraghty

Published in the United States of America by Crown
Publishers, Inc., a Random House company, 201 East 50th St.,
New York, NY 10022. Originally published in Great Britain in
1994 by Hutchinson Children's Books.

CROWN is a trademark of Crown Publishers, Inc.
Manufactured in Hong Kong

Library of Congress Cataloging-in-Publication Data
Geraghty, Paul.
The hunter / by Paul Geraghty.
p. cm.
Summary: After being separated from her grandfather in the
forest, a young African girl sees elephant poaching firsthand
when she rescues a baby elephant whose mother has been
killed by hunters.
[1. Africa—Fiction. 2. Elephants—Fiction. 3. Hunting—Fiction.
4. Grandfathers—Fiction.] I. Title.
PZ7.G293445Hu 1994
[E]—dc20 93-22730

ISBN 0-517-59692-X (trade)
       0-517-59693-8 (lib. bdg.)

10 9 8 7 6 5 4 3 2 1

First American Edition

In the early morning, Jamina went with her grandfather to collect honey. They followed the honey bird far into the bush.

"I want to see elephants!" Jamina cried. "Grandfather, do you think we will?"

"You'll be lucky if you do," said the old man. "We don't see many now. Not since the hunters came."

"Hunters!" Jamina's eyes lit up. "I'm going to be a hunter."

Jamina played hunter. She shot the mighty elephant; she tracked a rhino deep into the forest; she stalked a pride of lions.

Then she turned back to look for her grandfather. But she had wandered too far into the bush and the old man and the honey bird were nowhere to be seen.

She called out but there was only silence.

Then, far away on the wind, Jamina heard a sound. A sad and desperate cry that tugged at her heart. She held her breath and listened.

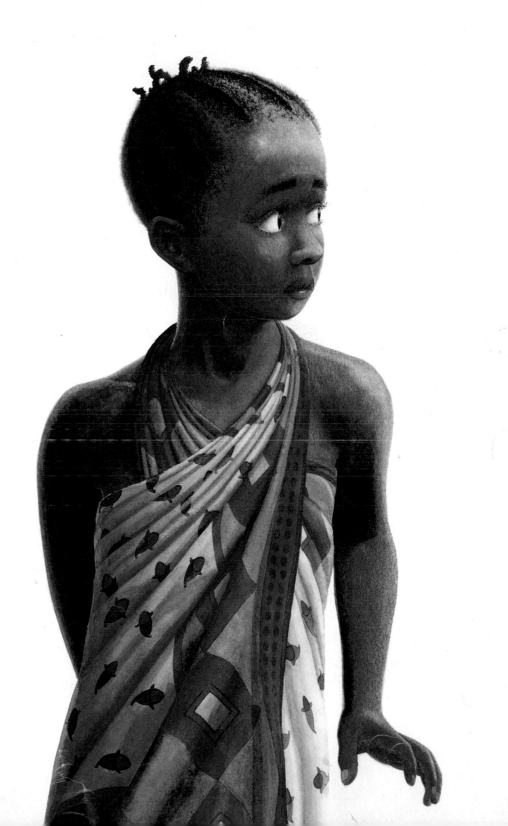

Jamina looked up. Vultures hung high in the heavy noon heat, and all around she could sense danger.

"Never go alone into the bush," her parents had warned. But the sound was so mournful she couldn't help but follow.
   Farther and farther she went ...

... until she came to a clearing. There she found a tiny elephant, trying in vain to wake his mother. The hunters had been there, and like Jamina, he was lost and afraid.

"Don't cry, little one," she whispered.

Jamina tilted her head to listen. Perhaps the rest of the herd was nearby. But all she could hear was the endless rasping of insects in the heat.

She knew the baby would not survive alone. She could try to lead him home with her, and perhaps they would find his family on the way.

   But the baby was frightened.

   "I am not a hunter," she said softly. For a long time she spoke to the elephant until he grew calm and nuzzled her with his trunk.

Jamina stood up and walked a few steps. The baby followed, tottering weakly in the blazing heat. Then the rain came, and cooled by the water, the elephant found strength to go on. At times they slipped and struggled, but they kept on walking, right through the storm.

As the skies cleared, the baby grew excited, and for a moment Jamina thought she could hear elephants. But when she stopped to listen, there was only the whispering of the wind in the grass. For a long time the elephant would not move. Then, sadly and silently, he walked on.

"If you are lost," her grandfather had told her, "follow the afternoon herds; they will lead you to the river. Home is on the other side."

It was a long time before Jamina and the elephant found the herd of zebra making its way across the plain. They traveled with the thirsty animals all through the hot afternoon.

As the sun dipped low in the sky, they finally reached the river. But hidden eyes watched them from the water, and Jamina sensed danger there.

"It is not safe to cross here, little one," she said. "We must travel on."
As Jamina turned, she thought she could see elephants on the horizon.
She blinked and strained her eyes, but there were only the acacia
trees, shimmering in the hazy heat.

Jamina and the elephant set off again, but soon the baby began to slow down.

"Just a little farther," begged Jamina. But he was too tired to go on. As Jamina waited with him, she thought of her mother. If only she could call her. Soon people would worry; soon they would come searching. The baby whimpered. She stroked him gently. He had no mother to call.

"Listen!" Jamina hushed the elephant. They could hear voices. My parents! she thought.

But the dark shadows in the distance were not her parents.

"Poachers!" she gasped under her breath. Now Jamina felt she, too, was one of the hunted. She prayed that the baby would not whimper. But the elephant sensed evil and stayed as still as a stone until the danger passed.

Darkness fell, and the whoops and howls of the night creatures echoed in the distance. Jamina huddled close to the baby, then clung to him in fear as the deep and terrifying groan of something hungry sounded nearby.

As she waited to be hunted, the words of her grandfather came to her again.

"If ever you are in danger," he had said, "never lose hope."

So Jamina listened for her parents. She closed her eyes and wished for them.

But instead she saw elephants. Her mind was filled with the great herds of long ago. Herds that her grandfather had seen when he was young. Mighty tuskers, whose shadows moved like ghosts across the plains.

   She could hear their deep and gentle murmurs close by.

When she opened her eyes, there were elephants all around, as if she'd called them in her dream. Jamina wasn't afraid.

"Take this little one," she said. "And keep him safe."

By the first light of dawn, Jamina's mother found her sleeping in the grass.

"I was playing hunter and I got lost," Jamina said. She stayed very close to her mother all the way home.

And as they reached the village, she said softly to herself, "I will never be a hunter."